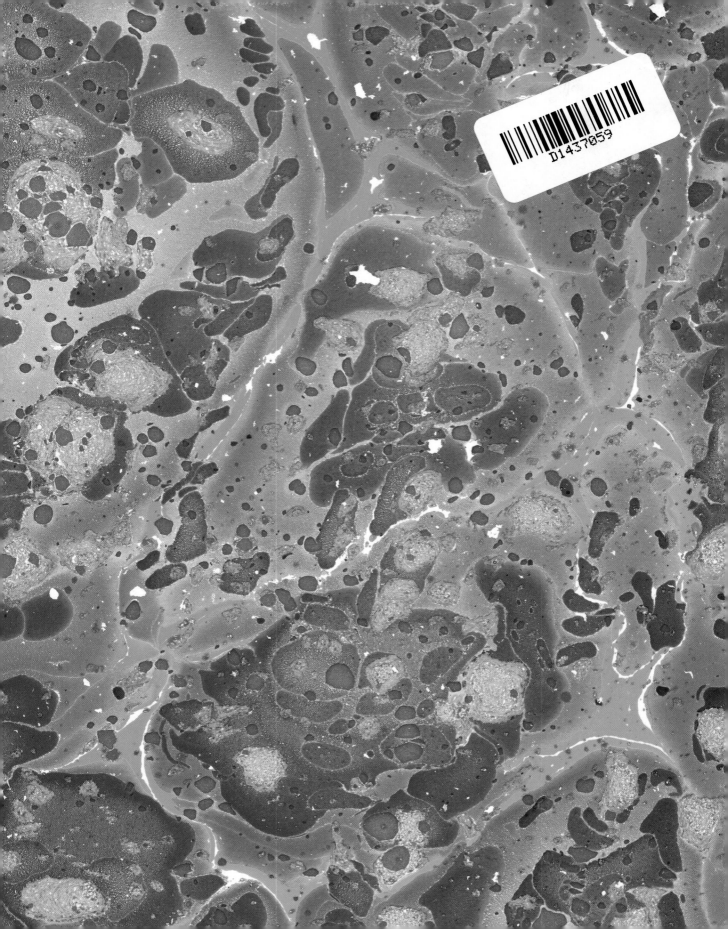

For my family

BLACKIE CHILDREN'S BOOKS

Published by the Penguin Group
Penguin Books Ltd, 27 Wrights Lane, London W8 5TZ, England
Penguin Books USA Inc., 375 Hudson Street, New York, New York 10014, USA
Penguin Books Australia Ltd, Ringwood, Victoria, Australia
Penguin Books Canada Ltd, 10 Alcorn Avenue, Toronto, Ontario, Canada M4V 3B2
Penguin Books (NZ) Ltd, 182-190 Wairau Road, Auckland 10, New Zealand

Penguin Books Ltd, Registered Offices: Harmondsworth, Middlesex, England

First published 1993
1 3 5 7 9 10 8 6 4 2

Made and printed in Hong Kong by Imago

A CIP catalogue record for this book is available from the British Library

ISBN 0 216 93252 1

The Wonderful Bag

Folk Tales of the World

An Arabian Tale from the Thousand & One Nights

Retold and Illustrated by

Gini Wade

Blackie Children's Books

One fine morning, Ali the Persian was sitting in his shop when Hamid, a big strong mountain man came by. He looked at some of the goods for sale and then, without warning, grabbed a small damask bag and walked away as calmly as if he had owned it since the day he was born.

Astonished, Ali ran after him, yelling, 'Give me back my bag, or else pay me good money for it!'

Hamid simply shrugged his shoulders and growled, 'This bag, and everything in it, belongs to me.'

In a fury, Ali shouted, 'O fellow Muslims, help me save my goods from this wretch!'

A large crowd of merchants and townsfolk instantly gathered round and advised, 'Go to the wise and all-seeing Kadi! He'll decide who is right and who is wrong.'

Many willing hands helped Ali drag Hamid through the market to the Hall of Judgement, where sat the Kadi.

'Which of you is laying the complaint?' he asked.

Before Ali had a chance to open his mouth, Hamid stepped forward saying, 'Allah bless my master the Kadi! This bag is *my* bag and everything in it belongs to me. I lost it and then by great good fortune saw it again in this man's shop.'

'In that case,' said the Kadi, 'to prove that it is yours, give me a list of its contents.'

Without a moment's hesitation, Hamid said, 'In my bag, O Kadi, there are two crystal flasks, a lamp with a djinn, fine Persian carpets, a cat with six kittens, three camels, two needles, a silver pin *and* fifty mountain men all ready to swear this bag is mine!'

Then the judge
turned to Ali, saying,
'What is your answer to this?'
Ali couldn't believe his ears. He
was so astonished by Hamid's
words, that it took him a little while
to come to his senses. At first all
he could say was, 'May Allah
lift up and honour our master
the Kadi. That hairy
wretch is a thief and
a liar!'

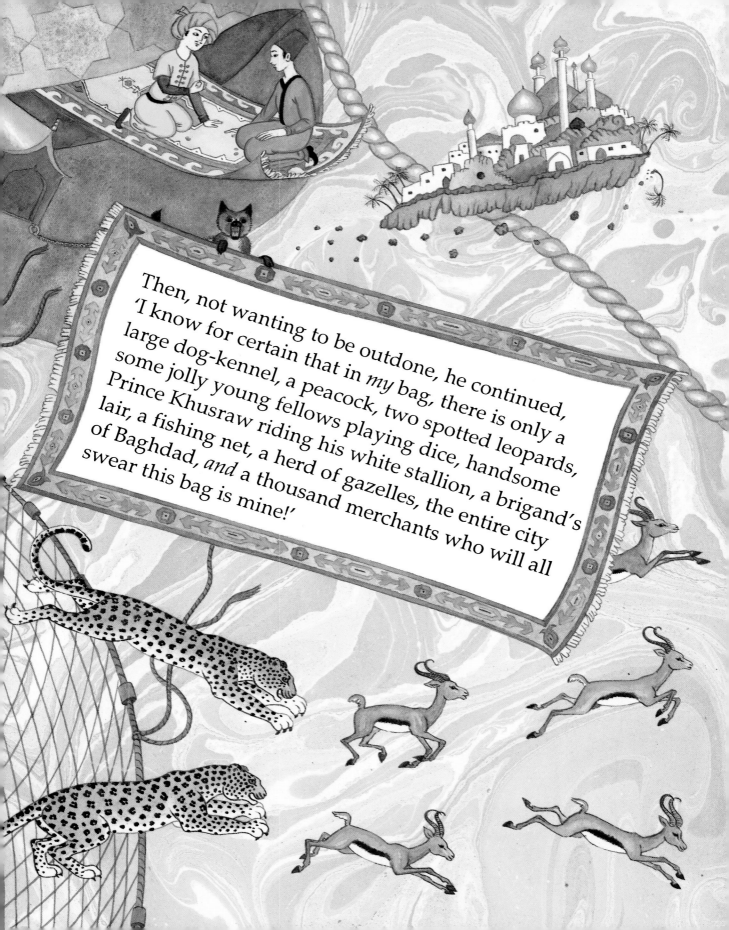

Then, not wanting to be outdone, he continued, 'I know for certain that in *my* bag, there is only a large dog-kennel, a peacock, two spotted leopards, some jolly young fellows playing dice, handsome Prince Khusraw riding his white stallion, a brigand's lair, a fishing net, a herd of gazelles, the entire city of Baghdad, *and* a thousand merchants who will all swear this bag is mine!'

Hamid had been
thinking hard while Ali was
speaking, and when Ali finished,
he burst into tears, and sobbed,
'O great Kadi! My bag is known
throughout the land! Ask anybody
who has eyes to see and a heart
to tell, and they will say
this bag belongs
to me.'

Hamid continued, 'As well as those things I have already mentioned, my bag contains an ivory chess set studded with emeralds and pearls, a mare and her foal, a golden scimitar, a sailing ship, ghouls and phantoms, two beautiful Greek slaves, an Abyssinian playing the clarinet, figs and apples, a chest full of golden dinars, the great mosque of Mashhad, a plank and a nail, the fabled palace of Suleiman the Magnificant, all the lands between Balkh and Isfahan, the Indies and Sudan, *and* - may Allah preserve the days of our master the Kadi - a shroud and a coffin for the Kadi if he does not say this bag is mine!'

The Kadi rose up at this in a great fury and thundered, 'By Allah! Either you are both rascals mocking myself and the holy law, or this bag is indeed a bottomless abyss filled with wonders! Whoever has been lying to me will be made to regret his piece of impudence. I shall now open the bag to see which one of you has been telling me the truth.'

The assembled crowd gasped and craned their necks for a better view, as the Kadi turned the bag upside down and shook it.

All that fell out was a shrivelled piece of orange peel, and some olive stones!

Ali looked on in dismay, and thought desperately for the last time. Finally he stammered, 'O Kadi, now I can tell, looking more closely at the bag, that the pattern of the damask is slightly different to mine. I don't know how I could have made such a mistake. This bag must belong to Hamid!' So saying, Ali turned smartly on his heel and left the Judgement Hall, leaving poor Hamid to the wrath of the Kadi and the disappointed crowd.

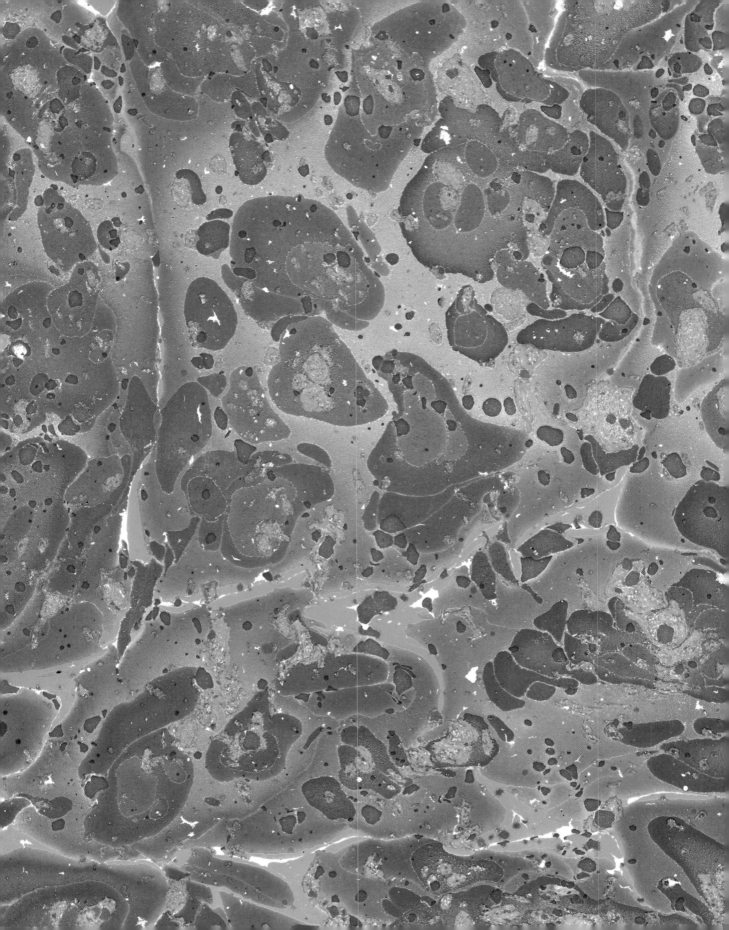